HORACE

by **HOLLY KELLER**

 Greenwillow Books, New York

*Watercolor paints and a black pen
were used for the full-color art.
The text type is Korinna.*

*Copyright © 1991 by Holly Keller
All rights reserved. No part of this book
may be reproduced or utilized in any form
or by any means, electronic or mechanical,
including photocopying, recording, or by
any information storage and retrieval
system, without permission in writing
from the Publisher, Greenwillow Books,
a division of William Morrow & Company, Inc.,
1350 Avenue of the Americas, New York, NY 10019.
Printed in Singapore by Tien Wah Press
First Edition   10 9 8 7 6 5*

Library of Congress Cataloging-in-Publication Data

*Keller, Holly.
Horace / by Holly Keller
p.   cm.
Summary: Horace, an adopted child, realizes
that being part of a family depends on
how you feel and not how you look.
ISBN 0-688-09831-2.
ISBN O-688-09832-0 (lib. bdg.)
[1. Parent and child—Fiction.
2. Adoption—Fiction.
3. Self-acceptance—Fiction.]
I. Title   PZ7.K28132Ho   1991
[E]—dc20   90-30750   CIP   AC*

FOR SUSAN

Horace lived in a small pink house with his parents.

He had his own room and his own toys. And every night at bedtime Mama told him the same story.

"We chose you when you were a tiny baby because you had lost your first family and needed a new one. We liked your spots, and we wanted you to be our child."

But Horace always fell asleep before Mama finished.

They were a fine family. Horace played checkers
with Papa every night, and Mama knit him special
slippers so his feet would never be cold.

Sometimes when Mama made Horace eat his oatmeal and brush his teeth, or Papa made him wear his boots, Horace wished for different parents. But most of the time he was happy.

Mama planned a party for Horace's birthday.

"All your cousins are coming," she told him.

Mama made Horace's favorite stew. She baked a big birthday
cake and everybody sang. But Horace was sad.

"My spots are silly," he said, looking around the table,

"and I'm all the wrong colors."

Later he tried to turn his spots into stripes, but it didn't work.

Then he cut some pictures out of magazines
and hung them on the wall.

That night Mama tucked Horace into bed.

She patted his back and told him the same story as always.

"We chose you when you were a tiny baby because you had
lost your first family and needed a new one. We liked your
spots, and we wanted you to be our child."

And, as always, Horace fell asleep before the end.

He dreamed about being someplace
where everybody looked like him.

In the morning he stuffed some money and a few things into his pillowcase. He left a note on the refrigerator.

The park seemed a good place to begin.

A traveling carnival had set up near the duck pond, and he
bought some cotton candy. He was glad not to have anyone
there to remind him that he would have to brush his teeth.

Then he got a ticket for the Ferris wheel.
"I'll be able to see everyone from the top," he told
the ticket man.
But when he looked down, everything was too small,
and his stomach felt awful.

The carnival was crowded, so Horace took the boat across the pond. He hummed a little song to help him feel brave. Then he saw them. A big family, all spotted just like him, was having a picnic under a tree.

Horace sat down on a bench and watched.
"Come and play with us," the littlest one called when
she noticed Horace sitting by himself.

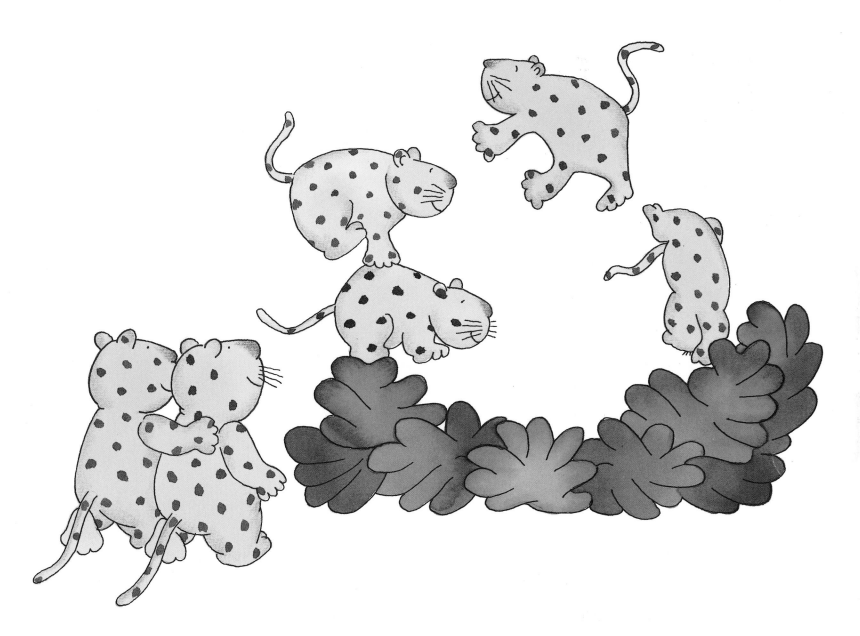

And Horace went to join the others.

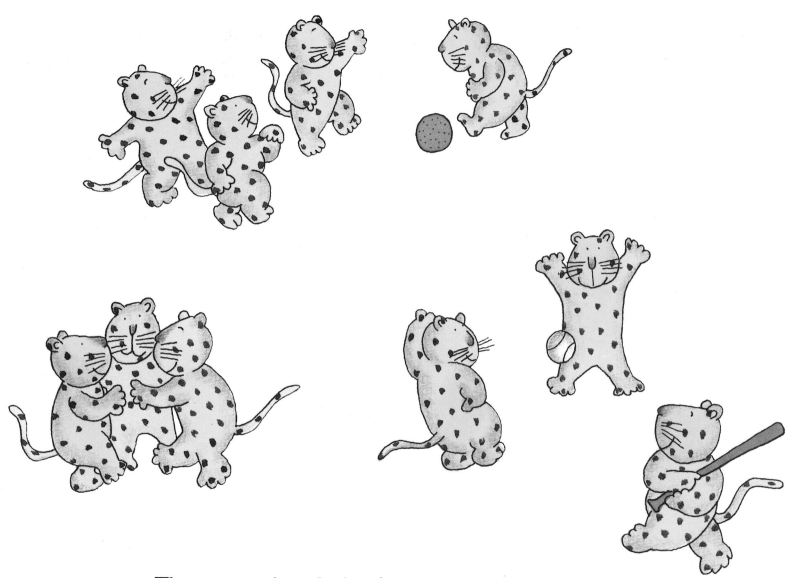

They spent the whole afternoon playing games.

Horace had fun, and he liked his new friends.

"Time for one more game before we go home," the mama called.

They played hide and seek. Horace hid behind a big rock.

He waited and waited.

The sun was going down and the air was chilly. Horace's feet felt cold.
He thought about his slippers. He wondered if Papa was waiting for him
to play checkers and if Mama missed him.

"Here he is!" somebody finally shouted, but
Horace didn't feel like playing anymore.
"Come with us," his new friends said. Horace shook his head.
"I want to go home now," he said.

Horace caught the last boat back across the pond.

The carnival was all shut down,
but Mama and Papa were there,
and they were looking for him.
In a flash he was in Mama's arms.

At bedtime Mama told Horace the story again. "We chose you
when you were a tiny baby because you had lost
your first family and needed a new one.
We liked your spots, and we wanted you to be our child."

And this time Horace listened all the way to the end.

"Mama," he said just before he closed his eyes,

"if you chose me, can I choose you, too?"

"That would be very nice," Mama said.

"Then I do," Horace whispered, and he was asleep.